Cultivating Lifelong Donors:
Stewardship and the Fundraising Pyramid

Authors

FRANK BARRY

LAWRENCE HENZE

DAVID LAMB

KATHERINE SWANK

2010

Editors: Heather Friedrichs Lyman & Lindsey Houston Salmony

TABLE OF CONTENTS

Major &
Planned Donors

Loyal &
Transition Givers

Small or
Occasional Donors

Supporters & Prospects

INTRODUCTION

by Lawrence Henze

The creation of a "complete" fundraising pyramid requires time and patience. Many years of experience in the fundraising world and significant statistical evidence demonstrate that "ultimate" donors with the greatest staying power are those acquired through the annual giving program and cultivated to become sustainable donors using good stewardship and best fundraising practices.

Nonprofit organizations need strategies for building giving programs from engagement up through ultimate giving, which requires taking a fresh look at strategies for engaging new supporters online, understanding the characteristics of loyal donors, developing personal relationships with transitional giving prospects, and exploring cultivation strategies that foster lifetime commitments. This exercise lays the groundwork for a fundraising pyramid that fulfills its promise and helps you maximize fundraising results.

Primarily relying on peer-based major giving programs can hamper the natural progression of sustainable donors up the fundraising pyramid when long-term strategies are not implemented to foster their cultivation through stewardship. Why? Because sustainable donors develop through the annual giving program and are cultivated over time, and there is plenty of statistical evidence to support this conclusion.

For example, my research shows that donors make $1,000 gifts to organizations most often when they have already been giving to the organization for about seven years. Long-term research with successful nonprofits also shows that those very same donors are approximately 900% more likely to make a major gift in their lifetime than individuals without that progressive history. Of course, there are experiential differences among organizations, but the trend is clear.

The reasons many low-end donors give for a year or two and then lapse are also based on a lack of stewardship. Acquisition is frequently based on the sole goal of increasing the number of annual donors, rather than the more appropriate goal of attracting sustainable donors. Plus, there is absolutely no foreseeable reason that individuals originally acquired through online or social media giving channels will mature any differently in the future provided that appropriate stewardship strategies are consistently practiced.

Yet another reason we do not develop enough major giving donors from our constituents is that many fundraising practices do little to promote transitional giving (the movement from annual giving donor to major giving prospect). Transitional giving prospects are often neglected in fundraising infrastructure and exist in "no-man's land" between annual giving and major giving staff.

It is clear that the answer to ultimate fundraising success does not lie in generating more peer-generated gifts that often disappear when the peer-solicitor leaves the organization or begins soliciting for another cause. Of course, these gifts should still be sought, but the theory that major donors come to organizations via other major donors doesn't actually hold up under analysis. And it is simply not a sustainable model for continued growth.

We need better ideas and a willingness to try different concepts and strategies. And we need cultivation strategies that foster personal investment in organizational goals, starting at the time of engagement and holding steady throughout a supporter's lifetime. Only then can we realize a fundraising pyramid that fulfills its promise.

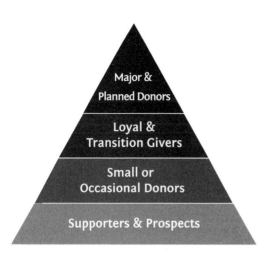

CHAPTER ONE

Engaging Donors Through Social Media
by Frank Barry

H aving a social media strategy is not an objective in itself. Rather, social media strategies can support your existing objectives. Reflect on your organization's current objectives: Do you want to cultivate supporter relationships, build cause awareness, do online fundraising, or connect with new supporters? These are all goals social media can help support. This chapter examines a multitude of ways to get started and how your organization can benefit by acquiring new prospective donors and building a deeper level of commitment with current supporters.

Your Social Media Strategy

You have a great framework: You acquire donors, cultivate them, and fundraise using both online and offline channels. But you have a nagging interest in social media. Newspapers and television shows are constantly referring to Twitter® and Facebook®, and the number of people participating in those channels is staggering. The first thing that strikes you is the potential for reaching large numbers of people. As you think about it more, the type of personalized, engaged, high-value relationships you could cultivate with people through social media becomes perhaps even more intriguing.

But how do you get started? You probably have these questions:

1. How can my organization use social media to pursue specific objectives?

2. What are the risks, and how can they be managed?

3. What are some examples of social media techniques that have provided real results?

4. How do we know what's being accomplished?

When did the Web Get Social?

Given all the talk about "social media," you might assume that the Web's core technology recently changed. But really (and of course), the Internet was conceived as a social medium. Email, the origination point for social computing, got started 39 years ago![1] Discussion groups and file sharing got started 30 years ago as USENET. "Talk," a real-time chat program like Yahoo! Messenger® and AOL Instant Messenger®, arrived on the scene 26 years ago. And the now venerable World Wide Web made its debut a full two decades ago.

So with these beginnings, why was the first Wikipedia® entry for "social media" not created until 2005? To see why this might be so, consider these two recent developments:

1. The Internet's ability to move and store large volumes of data has quintupled in the last decade.[2]

2. A majority of people in the U.S. now have a high-speed connection to the Internet in their homes.[3]

These two trends have created the technical and social environment needed for the original vision of the Internet as social medium to "go mainstream." And that's what's different: The Internet no longer could be social; now it actively is social!

The sheer number of people who enjoy and participate in social media makes it compelling. Your supporters and future supporters are out there, sharing photos, making connections, telling stories, giving advice, and watching videos:

○   More than 2.9 billion email accounts[4]

○   More than 400 million Facebook® users [5]

○   13 billion photos on Facebook® and Flickr® alone[6]

○   More than 161 million visits per month on Twitter®[7]

○   133 million blogs[8]

Go ahead, join them…they'll be glad to see you!

Build Cause Awareness: Bookmark Your Content — Socially!

Do you have anything on your website that you'd like to "boost"?

Social bookmarking is a method where Internet users can save and share bookmarks on public websites like Digg® or StumbleUpon®. Together, Digg® and StumbleUpon® serve more than 25 million unique visitors each month. The reason people use them is that they believe the community is a good judge of Web content: That is, if a lot of people have marked a web page as interesting or "digged" it, they might like it too.

Example
The National Wildlife Federation regularly submits content from its website to Digg® and StumbleUpon®. It was able to convert 243 "digs" into 43,703 page views for a web page that would have only received 4,834 page views without the social bookmarking "assist."[9] Visit http://digg.com/search?s=nwf.org to see the Federation's content.

Once your web page starts to gain popularity on a social bookmarking service, it can drive a tremendous amount of traffic back to your site and help spread awareness of your cause to thousands of potential supporters. Again, the numbers are huge: Digg® and StumbleUpon® serve more than 25 million unique visitors each month.

What It Takes

Submitting content is easy; you just need to create an account (i.e., a user profile), after which adding web pages to the site only takes a few seconds. What takes longer is developing the profile itself by spending some time each day participating in the social bookmarking community. You need to submit great quality items, but moreover, you need to rank other submissions, leave comments, and add friends to your network. The reason for this might not be clear until you notice two things:

o   Social bookmarking sites are "smart." They suggest content for you based on what people with similar profiles have liked. This matching engine will ultimately help your content reach many new people — but not until your profile has some usage data in it.

o   There is some social reciprocity at work (it is a social site after all). Some people will read an article you found interesting simply because you read an article they submitted.

Using social bookmarking, like many social media techniques, is "free" but does require an investment of time.

Measuring Results

Number of Page Views: Compare the amount of time you put into social bookmarking to the amount of money you would pay for an equivalent amount of online advertising.

Risk Management

Social bookmarking is a low-risk activity. Only submit the best content you have (as opposed to submitting everything). Then submit related high-quality content, and occasionally participate in the community by giving other submissions a "thumbs up." Following these simple guidelines will keep your profile in good standing.

Connect With New Supporters: Build a Facebook® Fan Page

A Facebook® page for your organization can help you enlist new supporters and provide you with demographic information about them. It allows you to have an interactive presence on a hugely popular social media site. Its functionality is more limited than your website, but it is easier to manage. With 400 million active users, it is structured in a way that directly helps you build your list of supporters. Additionally, your Facebook® page is a form of market research because of the demographic information it provides.

Example
Lance Armstrong Foundation was able to establish an additional way to communicate with more than 844,000 people by creating an organization page on Facebook®. Visit www.facebook.com/livestrong to see how they do it.

Another good example belongs to ONE, an advocacy organization committed to the fight against poverty and disease. Its Facebook® page, is www.facebook.com/one, is notable for its well-executed tie-in back to ONE's main website.

What It Takes

You can create a Facebook® page for your organization in just a few minutes by filling out this form: www.facebook.com/pages/create.php. Once your page is set up, you can control a whole host of powerful Web features, including discussion groups, photo galleries, and event promotions. Some tips to help you get started include:

○ Choose the setting that allows your followers to post to your fan page "wall."

○ Engage your fans by cross-posting blog content, as well as sharing pictures and videos on a regular basis; all of these have the potential to start conversations.

○ Regularly participate in the conversations happening on your fan page.

Measuring Results

○ Number of New Supporters: Count your fans as members of your house list. You can send these people messages through status updates on your Facebook® organization page.

○ Engagement of New Supporters: Treat your Facebook® page fans as a separate segment and compare their response rates to the response rates from other supporter groups in your list.

○ Supporter Demographics Report: Use the "Insights" tool to get activity, as well as demographic, data about your fans. You can then take that data and figure out which content is making the greatest impact.

Risk Management

Facebook® pages will allow you to choose whether or not fans can update your site with comments, links, photos, and videos. With these features turned off, there is almost no risk, but there is also almost no social or viral element. With these features turned on, you have approximately the same issue you have with a blog: What if someone makes an objectionable comment that is now appearing on your website property? Fortunately, Facebook® lets page administrators delete anything they don't like. As with blogs, it's best to create a short, clear policy and then enforce it consistently. Generally, excluding only hateful and obscene content is preferred; otherwise, you might lose a chance to connect with someone who is starting off with a different point of view but who may, through engagement, become a supporter.

Cultivate Relationships: Collaborate With Your Supporters

The Internet makes collaboration between large groups of widely spread people possible. And collaboration on substantive projects is great for building affinity in both directions — in your organization for its supporters, and in supporters for their organization.

Is there a way you could use the Internet to build affinity in your community through collaboration?

Example

In 2008, the Brooklyn Museum ran a program that engaged 3,344 people in a substantive, creative, and satisfying way. It created an exhibit called Click! where the public got to be both artist and jury. Through an online system, members of the Museum's web community submitted photographs and then selected those that would be included in the show. With such widespread involvement, the show was a great success.[10]

What It Takes

In the case described above, the core components were custom-built Web forms that allowed for the submission and review of the photographs. Both traditional and social media messaging channels would be a good fit for promotion.

Measuring Results

Comparative Engagement Measures: In the short term, you can measure the success of Click!-type initiatives in terms of how many people participate. Of additional interest is carefully comparing subsequent levels of engagement for your "collaborating" supporters to those of your general supporter population. Do they make donations or purchase memberships at the same rate? Do they renew memberships at the same rate? Rate differences could speak to the lasting effects of developing relationships through collaboration.

Risk Management

Social media risk usually centers on user-generated content. Blogs, photo galleries, and video libraries that users contribute to are clear examples of where this kind of risk could occur.

That said, user generated content is not a critical component of every social media strategy. In cases where it is (Click! for example), vetting before releasing the content for public consumption often eliminates the issue.

Build a Space on the Web for Just Your Community: Make a Private Social Network

When an organization wants to connect with its constituency in the context of a social network a Facebook® application, group or page is a great answer, right? After all, your people are likely already there. Of course, sometimes that isn't the whole story. In life and on the Web, people engage in different social realms and the huge, very-public, melting-pot that Facebook® represents isn't always a perfect fit if you are aiming to create an environment that is saturated with your group's unique character and whose functionality is specialized to your domain. Luckily, you can solve this problem without developing your own Facebook® from scratch; there are a number of great tools available to help you on your way.

Example
The United States Naval Academy Alumni Association and Foundation created an exclusive social network for alumni, parents, and friends that is a perfect fit for its unique community.

The organization found itself in exactly the situation described above and employed the User Networking Manager within Blackbaud® NetCommunity™ to quickly and effectively build USNA Connect, a specialized social network for Naval Academy alumni, parents and friends that is a perfect fit for its unique community. Facebook® still has its place in the organization's social media strategy in the form of a fan page with photos, videos, and articles, but USNA Connect is a unique site that reflects the camaraderie of the Naval Academy and it features a host of functions that were specifically designed for its users:

o "Suggested Friends": Tool suggests people you may know based on your friends and relationships in The Raiser's Edge®.

o "Your Events": Shows all of the events you are attending and a list of others also attending that event.

o "Friend Map": Displays a map overlaid with the locations of your friends in USNA Connect.

o "Class News": News feed of articles and blog posts related to your class.

o "Top Pages/News Articles": A listing of the most popular news articles and pages on their website.

What It Takes

Tools like Blackbaud® NetCommunity™ greatly simplify the task of building a private social network. The backend database along with all the foundational pieces of functionality needed for a social network are already provided. These building blocks give your members the ability to create personal profiles, send messages, make friends, form sub-groups, and upload photos to their accounts. Users can also link their profiles to their Facebook® accounts to allow easy picture sharing. That said, building your unique social network will still require a significant investment of time from your organization. Conceptualization, design, configuration, and customization will all be important steps in your process. For most groups, a network build will be a small team's primary focus for at least a quarter of the year.

Measuring Results

Penetration Rate: Often, a private social network's aim is to support and extend "connectedness" within a community of known size. Measure what percentage of your community is participating.

Activity Level: The question you want to ask after "What percentage of my community has joined?" is "How active are those who have?" If people are logging on, reading and making posts, creating friend-connections and sharing photos, you are well on your way to achieving your goals.

Risk Management

Lackluster Adoption: You don't want to consume your organization's resources building a network that doesn't get used. To mitigate this risk make sure your network reflects social patterns that already exist, or at least have tremendous potential to exist, in the offline world. Also, be realistic about the ongoing resource commitment your network will require: as "host" you need to introduce new content and ideas to facilitate continuous engagement and relevancy for your members.

Objectionable User Generated Content: Private social networks can have an advantage with respect to objectionable content because they are often populated by a group that already shares a similar set of values and sensibilities. Also, the members are far less anonymous to one another than they might be in more disjoint networks like MySpace®. The result is that these groups usually don't need much policing and will keep each other "in bounds" effectively. For your part, just be sure to provide links that allow people to flag or report suspect content so that it can be reviewed.

Five Steps to Start Leveraging Social Media

1. **Pick an Existing Goal to Pursue.** Identify something your organization wants to accomplish. Many organizations find that social media provides good support for:

- Building cause awareness
- Connecting with new supporters
- Soliciting online gifts
- Cultivating supporter relationships

   If you are just starting, pick one of these to focus on and let that objective guide you every step of the way.

2. **Make Success Someone's Job.** Or at least make it an explicit part of someone's job! Treat social media like you would your other communication channels: Figure out where responsibility for your social media programs should reside in your organization and assign responsibility. Making an overt assignment (like you probably do with direct mail, email, telemarketing, public relations, and advertising) will let a person or group of people

on your staff develop the focus, comprehensive view, and skills needed to leverage these new techniques effectively.

3. **Listen.** With your team identified and an initial goal in mind, you might be tempted to jump right in. Resist, at least until you have two more pieces in place: the ability to listen in the social media channels and a baseline presence you can use as a foundation for your subsequent social media campaigns.

   There are three good reasons for listening:

   o Social media is a two-way channel. As politeness prescribes, you need to be ready to listen before you add to the conversation.

   o Organizations like yours are already participating. Looking at what they've done will give you inspiration, cautionary information, and a sense of what you need to do to differentiate your organization.

   o Once you do start to contribute content, the disciplined framework for listening you've put in place will be used to measure the reach and impact of your initiatives.

   Here are some ways to regularly monitor and listen to your social media channels:

   o Use the flexible automated alerts through Google® to receive periodic emails listing mentions of your organization across a variety of different types of Web content: www.google.com/alerts.

   o Search for your organization's name (or topic words) being used in the micro-blogging world with the search portal on Twitter®: www.search.twitter.com.

   o Track the number of times a blog mentions your organization or related topics at www.technorati.com.

   o Track the number of mentions for your organization's name, your staff, and events you are currently running in each of these mechanisms. This will help measure your organization's current social media footprint and prepare you to measure the reach of your future initiatives.

4. **Establish a Baseline Social Media Presence.** After establishing your organization's ability to "listen" in the social media channel, the next step is to establish a baseline presence you can use as a foundation for your subsequent social media campaigns. Remember, the places you choose to engage should be places that make sense based on your objective.

   First, create an organization Facebook® page. This will provide an outlet for any of the more than 400 million Facebook® users who may want to connect with your organization on Facebook® in a social way. The first version of your page can be very simple, and you can launch it in minutes. To get started, it doesn't need to do much more than greet your supporters and provide a link back to your website.

   Second, create a Twitter® account. This will give your organization a voice to speak with in the micro-blogging world. To get started, send out updates about newly available Web resources, events, or programs your supporters will be interested in. Include links to the root content on your website.

5. **Evolve.** Now you have an objective, dedicated staff, a way to listen and to measure results, as well as a foundational presence in the social media landscape. Reflect on what you've learned in your first few weeks of watchful monitoring, review the program examples talked about in the "Pursing Objectives" section above, and formulate the plan for your first social media campaign. Your supporters are out there waiting to engage. Ready? Go!

[1] Raymond Samuel Tomlinson invents email: http://openmap.bbn.com/~tomlinso/ray/firstemailframe.html

[2] http://www.nytimes.com/2009/06/14/magazine/14search-t.html?pagewanted=all

[3] http://www.usatoday.com/tech/news/2009-06-03-internet-use-broadband

[4] http://www.radicati.com/wp/wp-content/uploads/2010/04/Email-Statistics-Report-2010-2014-Executive-Summary2.pdf

[5] http://mashable.com/2010/02/04/facebook-400-million/

[6] http://mashable.com/2008/10/15/facebook-10-billion-photos/
http://en.wikipedia.org/wiki/Flickr

[7] http://siteanalytics.compete.com/twitter.com/

[8] http://technorati.com/blogging/state-of-the-blogosphere/

[9] http://www.slideshare.net/kanter/social-media-roi-case-study-slam-traffic

[10] http://www.brooklynmuseum.org/exhibitions/click/quick_facts.php

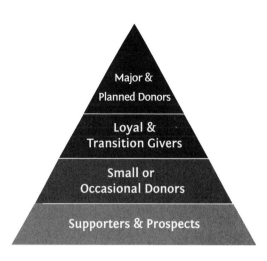

CHAPTER TWO

Stewarding "One-Time" Donors for Lasting Support
by David Lamb

In the wake of disasters or other monumental events, many people who do not regularly donate to nonprofits are moved to help by making one-time gifts. New donors rise to the occasion and flood nonprofit databases. Is there a way to capture this show of ardent emotion, and what can be done to kindle those sparks of compassion into flames of ongoing philanthropy? Indeed, there is…it's called stewardship.

Retaining new donors is not a trivial challenge. Let's explore the example of giving following a natural disaster.

Giving to disaster relief is often an emotional decision — it is impulse philanthropy. Today, the impulse to give is enhanced by the dramatic growth in technologies that facilitate donations for disaster relief: cell phone text giving, web donations, and multi-media publicity (including traditional media plus Twitter®, Facebook®, and other social media). Spurred by heart-wrenching images from disaster scenes, hundreds of thousands of new donors use these technologies to lend their aid. However, retention of these "disaster donors" usually falls off precipitously in the months following the disaster. As Giselle Holloway, director of direct response for the International Rescue Committee based in New York, said, "A person doesn't truly become a donor until they make their second gift."[1] That is to say, a donor's connection to your organization is tenuous at best until he or she becomes a repeat donor.

Sometimes the inflow of disaster donations creates a unique problem: too much money earmarked for a specific purpose. Often, disaster-specific donations coming in large numbers in a short timeframe can exceed an organization's ability to spend the money effectively for the intended purpose. This creates a different kind of stewardship problem. The danger is that, in an effort to honor the donors' intent, the nonprofit may spend the money unwisely or ineffectively.

The American Red Cross historically resolved this problem by taking donations given in response to one disaster and banking them against future disasters. This was a rational approach and helped the organization prepare for the unknown, but it was not widely or well understood by many of the donors. This business model became publicized during the Katrina disaster and brought a great deal of negative publicity. Under pressure, the Red Cross adopted a policy of double-checking with donors who did not earmark their donations to make sure they understood their gifts were going to a general fund instead of a specific crisis.

The clear answer — and the challenge for donor stewardship — is to convert impulse donors who respond compassionately to an emergency into long-term donors who help the organization to prepare for future emergencies. However, experience suggests that most of these will not become ongoing supporters of these organizations. They are primarily one-time donors — or periodic emergency-only donors. Nevertheless, an effective post-disaster stewardship plan may help convert some who would otherwise fall away into repeat donors.

Personalizing Your Stewardship

Let's start with the basics. You will certainly not retain your donors — no matter how they are acquired — if you do not give them a timely acknowledgement. Although an IRS-compliant receipt is a must, it's a good idea to respond back as personally as you can to the donors in the same way they initially reached out to you. Did they give through a Facebook® donation page? Invite them to become members of your Facebook® organization page to keep up with the latest things you are doing. Did they give through a telephone solicitation? Follow up with a phone call — even if it's only robo-calling.

*You will certainly not retain your donors —
no matter how they are acquired — if you do not give them a
timely acknowledgement.*

Personalize the acknowledgements as much as possible. Use the donor's name and reference the purpose to which the gift was given. And since the donor is particularly interested in that specific purpose, let your acknowledgement provide the donor feedback about what his or her gift accomplished in human terms — people sheltered, treated, and fed, for example. Tell the story of those who benefited from the donor's generosity.

Although it is acceptable — and probably expected — that your initial acknowledgement will include some kind of ask for additional support, it is best that this be a soft ask through inclusion of a donation card or insert. Your initial contact after the donation should be primarily focused on welcoming the donor to your organization and educating them on your mission. Most advisors suggest that you not wait too long before you do make the next ask, but the advice here is to let your thank-you be sincere and simple.

Mission Focus

Stewardship materials give you an opportunity to expand the story beyond what happened in the immediate aftermath of the disaster at hand to the larger mission of your organization. Often, impulse donors don't know a great deal about what else the nonprofit they supported does. This is your chance to make the case for ongoing support. Ideally, you want to convert these first-time donors into those who provide sustaining support, enabling your organization to be quick in responding to future disasters. Your goal is to make these supporters feel like partners with you in fulfilling your overall mission instead of just one-time donors.

With mission in mind, it must be said that if your organization's mission has nothing to do with disaster or other emergency relief, it is unethical to accept donations designated for that purpose. However, many organizations with a humanitarian focus may not have disaster relief as their primary purpose, but may be in a position to offer relief nonetheless. For example, CARE USA, whose mission is to fight poverty, received tens of thousands of new donors who gave their first gift online following the Indonesian tsunami in 2004. Although disaster relief is not specifically what they do, the organization is well equipped provide support to people in crisis.

After previous emergencies, CARE's approach was to thank new donors and put them in the normal direct mail system. Historically, their retention of these new donors was very poor. However, they tried a new approach with the tsunami donors. They created a stewardship program specifically for these people. Their message to them was: "Poverty is the Silent Tsunami."

"This strategy aimed to gain support for any poverty that makes people susceptible to crisis," said Adam Hicks, CARE's vice president for marketing and communications.[2] It highlighted the mission of the organization while engaging donors on the level of the crisis that brought them to CARE in the first place.

In this context, we need to also keep in mind a strategy to draw periodic donors closer. Some people give repeatedly, but only in response to catastrophic events. For a certain proportion of those who have historically given this way, this will never change. However, each new donation gives you a new chance to tie the donor more closely to what you do. In your acknowledgement, mention what they have given to before and how (and who) their past donations have helped. This is your chance to make the case that, since they have demonstrated trust in your organization multiple times in the past, they can make you even more effective in the future by establishing a regular giving pattern. They can become partners with you in preparing for the inevitable disasters to come rather than simply reacting on a case-by-case basis.

> *This is your chance to make the case that, since they have demonstrated trust in your organization multiple times in the past, they can make you even more effective in the future by establishing a regular giving pattern.*

Strategic Stewardship

Given the huge numbers of new and occasional donors who give in the aftermath of a disaster, it may not be possible to give the same level of highly personalized stewardship to every person. While all donors deserve a thank-you note and a receipt for their gift, a little extra attention may be warranted with some more than others.

There are several ways to segment your population for special attention, with one based on gift size. For donors to Katrina relief, there was a correlation between gift size and household income. Household incomes of more than $80,000 had median gift sizes of $100 and average gift sizes of $241.[3] This immediately suggests a strategy of allocating your more personal and more costly stewardship resources to donors at these higher levels.

Another strategy for prioritizing your stewardship resources is to respond to people, not only on the basis of their actual gift size, but also on the basis of their capacity to give, even if their actual gift is small. But how can you know someone's capacity? This requires some additional analysis. Use data mining techniques to discover the characteristics of your best existing donors. Do they tend to live in certain counties or ZIP codes? New or occasional donors from those same ZIP codes may be similar to your best donors in other ways, including the capacity to make continuing and larger gifts. If you have performed a statistical analysis of your donor population (modeling) prior to the disaster, it may be possible to use that analysis as a filter to help you prioritize some of your new and occasional donors for special attention.

Finally, don't wait until disaster strikes to create your stewardship plan. Disasters will come. Emergencies do happen. Gifts may begin to come in almost immediately. Make key decisions ahead of time so that your donor response is as effective as your relief efforts. Have letter, email, and website templates ready to go so that you can quickly communicate with your new donors without having to compose copy from scratch. The messages in these templates should focus on your organization's mission, with blanks where you can insert language specific to the emergency at hand.

Build the following seven steps into your plan:

1. Acknowledge new donors as soon as possible as personally as possible.

2. When practical, respond to them through the same channel (social media, direct mail, phone call) they used to reach you.

3. Let your stewardship materials tell the stories of those who were helped.

4. Use stewardship materials to expand your message beyond the immediate crisis to a description of your larger mission.

5. Engage new donors as partners in that mission.

6. If you can't provide the same level of stewardship to all constituents, prioritize prospects based on gift size or criteria you establish through data mining and modeling.

7. Prepare your stewardship plan before the disaster strikes.

By following these recommendations, you stand a much better chance of retaining more of the large influx of donors that give during a crisis.

---

[1] http://gettingattention.org/articles/66/strategies-campaigns/communicate-fundraise-crisis.html

[2] Tom Pope, "Converting Donors: How to Retain Donors from Disaster Solicitations", *Nonprofit Times*, February 15, 2006

[3] http://www.philanthropy.iupui.edu/Research/Giving/Disaster%20Giving%205-29-06.ppt

CHAPTER THREE

Transitional Giving for Building Strong Fundraising Pyramids

by Lawrence Henze

One of the best ways to realize the promise of your organization's fundraising pyramid is to strengthen its middle levels by promoting the growth of transitional and mid-level giving.

Just as the Egyptian pyramids have stood the test of time by standing strong from 3200 B.C. until the present day, you want your organization's fundraising pyramid to endure. A study of the pyramidal structure reveals that, in addition to the strong foundation, the middle of a pyramid is powerful itself; if the middle and top levels were removed and placed in the desert sands, they would be able to stand on their own. Would your fundraising pyramid achieve the same result? Most likely, the answer is "no."

Fortunately, the fundraising pyramid is not one of the Seven Wonders of the World, so I wouldn't risk international outcry if I suggested that we revisit its construction. And unless the pharaohs needed fundraising pyramids and campaigns to complete these massive undertakings, the historical precedent is lacking as well.

So, let's take a look at the concepts of transitional and mid-level giving, your fundraising pyramid, and strategies that could strengthen its core.

Transitional and Mid-Level Giving Defined

The concepts of transitional and mid-level giving are not interchangeable, although they are very similar, and both are desirable goals for donor growth. Both types of giving frequently encompass consistent or loyal giving.

Transition is defined in the *Merriam Webster Online Dictionary* as "a movement, development, or evolution from one form, stage, or style to another." Transitional giving, then, is the progression of a donor from entry-level giving through mid-level giving to ultimate giving. It is the outcome that we desire when a prospect first becomes a donor, but it is an outcome that does not happen as often as we would like. Later in this chapter, we will discuss how we can improve the chances of donors becoming ultimate givers.

Transitional giving, then, is the progression of a donor from entry-level giving through mid-level giving to ultimate giving. It is the outcome that we desire when a prospect first becomes a donor, but it is an outcome that does not happen as often as we would like.

Not surprisingly, mid-level giving is not defined in the dictionary; however, the word "textcasm," which is "sarcasm used in text messaging," has recently been added to *Merriam Webster's Open Dictionary*. If this were a chapter on social networks and fundraising, that aside may be more relevant, but alas, it is not.

Since we lack an official resource or document that defines the phrase "mid-level giving," I will provide a definition that I have come to know as a widely accepted one in the nonprofit world. Mid-level giving is the level of contributions that bridge the gap between annual and major giving. It may — or may not — lead to ultimate giving. In some instances, mid-level giving may reach a plateau, and donors will not transition to a higher level. In other instances, these donors will reach their ultimate giving level through a planned gift.

Both mid-level and transitional donors populate an area of the fundraising pyramid that is critical to your fundraising success. Finding more major giving prospects is best accomplished through internal data mining of existing donors rather than through acquisition.

Peer-to-peer donors, often the result of board members soliciting friends, are important but limiting. We rely on this fundraising method, in my opinion, because it is a short-term respite to a perpetual problem: the need for more major gift prospects. There is no reason, however, to abandon a course with far greater potential, as it is possible to pursue both options.

To better understand the need for transitional and mid-level gifts, let's take a look at your fundraising "pyramid."

What Shape Is Your Fundraising Pyramid?

It is a curious question, because the question itself suggests the answer. The truth is that the fundraising pyramid represents a concept as much as a shape, and it is highly likely that your pyramid does not resemble the traditional model. If you have any doubt, use a gift chart to build your own pyramid that represents your organizational reality.

Figure I shows an organizational pyramid that differs significantly from the traditional model and is likely to be closer to your reality. The wide base narrows very quickly to resemble a radio tower, if not a flagpole, and it only takes a quick observation to note that there are not enough prospects at the mid-level range to support growth at the top of the pyramid.

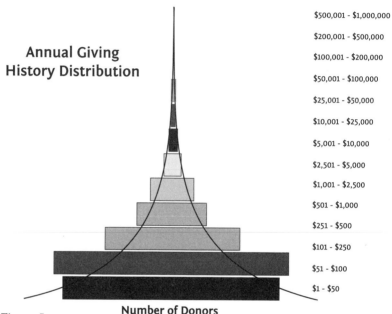

Figure I

If you accept the industry standard that you need at least three or four prospects for every capital campaign prospect, you can envision a scenario created by the donor distribution shown in *Figure I* in which your organization relies on the same top prospects for a long time. This is a primary reason that donor fatigue is a bigger issue than ever before. Ongoing capital campaigns compound the problem. To counter this issue, we need to change the "top-down" perspective for major prospect identification and adopt a strategy that concentrates on building our best donors through progressive movement up a wider donor pyramid.

To accomplish this goal, we must return to fundraising fundamentals that you may have set aside during your pressurized pursuit of current funds.

Who Are You?

For young readers and those not enamored with the CSI television series franchise, "Who Are You" is a song performed by the English rock band The Who. We can use its basic question as a guide as we consider who our prospects are and how we can identify those who are capable of mid-level and transitional gifts.

In general, transitional and mid-level donors exhibit a loyal pattern of giving — 60% of the time or more — and show upward trends in their giving over a period of time, such as five years or more. So, you may start identifying prospects by comparing their current giving levels compared to three or five years ago. "Wait a minute," you say. "I already do that!" True, it is basic Fundraising 101 as applied to identifying prospects with upgrade potential, and hopefully you practice it already. If not, it is an easy fix. You may start by looking for loyal donors with recent gifts that exceed their first gift in a designated time period, such as five years.

But we want to go beyond the obvious and uncover the more subtle characteristics that identify mid-level and transitional prospects. For that, let us turn to data mining. Depending on your interests, available resources, and the time constraints you operate under, you may or may not be able to fulfill all of the following steps.

Step 1: First, you'll need to define what range of giving constitutes "mid-level" for your organization. Armed with the data from the pyramid construction project demonstrated earlier, you have the donor distribution of your file. Now apply your knowledge of your current solicitation practices to identify the gift level/ask amount that triggers a high-touch contact, such as personalized annual fund or assignment of prospects to development officers. Let the data and your experience drive the range and not the benchmarking of your mid-level range against peer institutions. It is far more important to establish a reasonable range and then expand the number of donors giving within that range, as this will increase the likelihood that more donors will transition to higher levels in the future.

Step 2: Once you have identified individuals in the established mid-level range, you'll need to take a look at commonly held characteristics using single variable (also known as univariate) analysis. For example, you may want to determine how many years your mid-level donors contributed before donating at the mid-level range. If you have access to age data, you may want to first determine the average age at which mid-level giving commences and compare it to the average age that those same donors make their first gifts.

Figure II

Figure II compares years of annual giving to number of mid-level donors. From here you can easily calculate the average amount of time — 8.5 years — between first gift and mid-range gift. Now that you know the average gestation period, you may create a strategy that once donors reach five years of giving, you will treat them as mid-level prospects and implement high-touch cultivation and stewardship activities to increase the chances he or she will raise contributions to mid-level. You may further segment this pool to place a higher priority on individuals with an ascending trajectory in giving.

Similarly, with the earlier example that compared the average age at first gift to the average age at first mid-level gift, you can use that data to determine at what time in a donor's life he or she will begin to transition to a mid-level prospect. As mentioned above, use higher touch cultivation strategies to increase the "engagement" of these prospects and realize a higher mid-level conversion rate.

The previous examples focus on univariate analysis of internal data. Outside of your database, there is a rich selection of external attributes that you may add to your file to enhance your data mining activities. Let's start with "cluster" data.

Cluster data has been available for a long time, but the original services were limited by available data sources, and they aggregated households into larger geo-demographic groupings, such as ZIP codes or block groups. In recent years, however, the cluster services that are provided through Equifax's Niches, Acxiom's PersonicX®, and Nielsen's PRIZM® offerings have been compiled at the household level, and the resulting data is far more descriptive.

Cluster codes essentially group households by commonly held behavioral and marketing statistics that denote information such as likely buying behavior, household composition, and hobbies and recreational interests. Since we use Niche data at Blackbaud, I will use this service as an illustration. Equifax creates 26 Niches ranging from the young and wealthy "Already Affluent" Niche to the least prosperous "Zero Mobility" Niche. These clusters provide a picture of your prospects and donors and make it easier to craft the kind of targeted communications that make people feel as if you are talking to them individually.

To use the Niche clusters, you append the data to your file and begin to segment your database by the distribution of your mid-level donors through the 26 available scores, ranging from A-Z. For discussion purposes, let's randomly choose four clusters — A, B, D, and I — and say that we observe that 75% of your mid-level donors fall into these four categories. A logical next step is to determine whom among your constituents not already making mid-level contributions also fits into one of these Niches and is not yet giving or is giving at levels below mid-range. The latter group constitutes an upgrade population, and the former non-donor segment cries out for a different cultivation and solicitation strategy. We know from years of data analysis and client experience that many prospects never give because they are asked to engage at a lower level of giving. Furthermore, now that you have the appended clusters available to you, you can determine the clusters that correlate strongly with non-donors and use this information to reallocate your annual and mid-level giving resources to the segments most likely to bear fruit.

Finally, an added benefit of cluster data is that it may provide insights into messaging and potential channels of communication.

We know from years of data analysis and client experience that many prospects never give because they are asked to engage at a lower level of giving.

Step 3: As seen above, univariate analysis provides insights into the characteristics of your mid-level and transitional donors, albeit one attribute at a time. If you want to predict which of your prospects is most likely to make a transitional gift, for example, statistical modeling is the answer. Predictive or custom modeling allows you to drill down in your database to discover the best prospects, and the scoring mechanism enables you to adjust the number of prospects according to your resources and capacity. I have written on the subject of predictive modeling in my white paper *Using Statistical Modeling to Increase Donations*, which is available at www.blackbaud.com/whitepapers.

I strongly encourage you to consider using a specific statistical model that identifies transitional giving prospects. The model I recommend is based on donors who have transitioned through mid-level giving and have reached the major giving threshold. The prospects identified through this model will give you immediate potential in the mid-level and long-term possibilities for major giving. *Figure III* illustrates the potential expansion of prospects in the mid to upper levels of your pyramid.

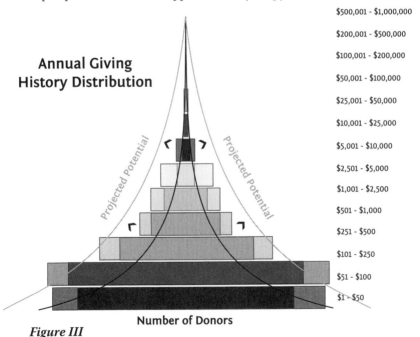

Annual Giving History Distribution

$500,001 - $1,000,000
$200,001 - $500,000
$100,001 - $200,000
$50,001 - $100,000
$25,001 - $50,000
$10,001 - $25,000
$5,001 - $10,000
$2,501 - $5,000
$1,001 - $2,500
$501 - $1,000
$251 - $500
$101 - $250
$51 - $100
$1 - $50

Number of Donors

Figure III

The matrix in *Figure IV* illustrates an example of a score distribution for two models: TGL (transitional giving likelihood) and TGR (target gift range). In the upper right corner, the prospects with the highest likelihood and target gift ranges are identified. For the organization used in this example, with a mid-level range of $1,001 to $5,000, the staff members now know who these prospects are and have a ready list of individuals who have the capacity to transition to major giving now.

TGL	TGR				
	$1-$250 (1,2,3)	$251-$500 (4)	$501-$1,000 (5)	$1,001-$5,000 (6,7)	>$5,000 (>=8)
>= 851+ (Excellent)	512	757	950	930	362
651-800 (Very Good)	2,060	412	192	106	51
551-650 (Good)	6,828	1,233	567	352	159
451-550 (Average)	9,583	1,331	580	381	164
<= 450 (Below Avg.)	19,714	1,546	722	380	128

Figure IV

Walking the Walk — Cultivating, Soliciting, and Stewarding Mid-Level and Transitional Giving Prospects

Once you commit to enhancing your mid-level program, you should also commit to reviewing your current policies for cultivation, solicitation, and stewardship. There is a good chance that your cultivation tactics may be too impersonal, your solicitations too frequent, and your stewardship overly targeted at the top of the pyramid to make it happen. Let's begin by reviewing strategies that could work more effectively.

1. A review of the giving pyramid for your organization gives you an idea of the level of support you can attain through maintaining the status quo. Data mining reveals additional potential and suggests that the status quo is not the route to pursue to cultivate and close those prospects. So change is needed, and ideally, it is change that can occur with minimal budgetary impact. If you accept this logic you will be poised for improvement.

2. Since you want to change the status quo, you need to understand what it really is, and the first area you want to understand is the frequency of contact with our constituents, the balance of the content of these contacts, and the channels you use for communication. You'll need to complete a communications audit, and it can easily be a do-it-yourself project.

   You should start with a goal of completing a comprehensive spreadsheet of your communications with your constituents, but you should start with the area that you work in: fundraising or advancement. First, you should determine how many times annually you solicit, inform, invite, and thank. If other units within your institution also contact constituents, you should add those contacts to the spreadsheet. You should plot these communications on a monthly calendar or spreadsheet.

   You should not be surprised if you discover that you communicate far more regularly than you imagined. Now you should look for communications that overlap in purpose and in timing and consolidate and eliminate. In doing so, you will be freeing budget resources for higher touch cultivation and reducing the intrusion in the lives of your donors and prospects, and that is exactly your intent!

3. Next, you should reach out to mid-level, transitional, and perhaps ultimate gift prospects identified through data mining to get an

understanding of their interests and preferences. In surveying your prospects, you should ask them to identify how they would like to hear from your organization and what their primary interests are within the context of your mission. Of course, you will not receive responses from many of the individuals, but the data gleaned from those who responded is invaluable. When you act upon it, you are likely to see an increase in engagement and support from the respondents. Then you can compile a report of the survey findings to share with your constituents; it will demonstrate your interest in their participation.

4. Since you have committed to reviewing the status quo and changing it to fit your new goals, you should review your solicitation policies for mid-level prospects. You will want to cultivate more often than solicit, so if you see that these prospects are asked multiple times annually for support, you should consider implementing a strategy of fewer, higher touch communications designed to promote engagement. You should recruit development and institutional staff, volunteers, and board members and involve them in the thanking process. And you should hold small thank-you events hosted by other donors to thank as well as disseminate information on the current and future plans for your organization and its mission.

5. While you are looking at solicitation policies, you should compile a list of fundraising priorities that may be shared with your prospects. As you move up the donor pyramid, you will encounter more prospects that will want to restrict their increased gifts, and it is best to be prepared.

6. Finally, your internal commitment should be to maximize the number of personal contacts you have with identified prospects. Each of your organization's staff members should seek time in their daily or weekly schedules that they can commit to

cultivation and solicitation. You should review each and every one of your recurring activities and determine if it is vital to growing our fundraising pyramid. If not, why are you doing it?

In conclusion, the Egyptians and other pyramid-building cultures took the logical approach to building pyramids by starting from the base and building upwards. Fundraisers, when facing campaigns and tight deadlines, have often built fundraising pyramids from the top-down and find that, after the campaign ends, there are precious few new prospects for the next campaign. Our research indicates that there are lessons to be learned from the ancient Egyptian civilization. If we build our funding support from the bottom up and emphasize a strong core, we will have development operations that can stand the test of time.

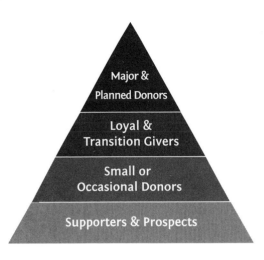

Major &
Planned Donors

Loyal &
Transition Givers

Small or
Occasional Donors

Supporters & Prospects

CHAPTER FOUR

Peak Performance: Strategic Stewardship for Planned Giving Programs
by Katherine Swank

When was the last time you personally spoke to the people who are leaving gifts to your organization in their wills? Was it more than three months ago? Longer? Never?! With the average bequest in the U.S. hovering between $35,000 and $70,000 and at around $30,000 in Canada, you can't afford to alienate your planned gift[1] donors.

True donor stewardship begins before you know that a gift has been made and continues even after the donor has passed away. A simple, yet strategic stewardship program welcomes your legacy[2] givers into the organization's highest ranks and provides them with a two-way relationship throughout their lives. Building an intentional bond with these future major donors improves your chances of receiving increased gifts from them now, as well as increased or additional legacy gifts in the future.

Consider this: As few as 15 people have the ability, when combined, to provide your organization with more than a million dollars![3] Are you making the time to incorporate best practices for planned gift donor recognition[4] and expanding your efforts to provide spectacular stewardship?

A View from the Top

Every fundraising professional eventually becomes acquainted with the fundraising pyramid. It's an effective visual aid that provides a solicitation continuum from entry-level donor to ultimate donor. Both major and planned gift donors reside at the peak of the pyramid and will be your organization's transformational contributors.

As we work through a traditional donor giving life-cycle with these individuals, stewardship becomes the linchpin — the central cohesive element on which other gifts hinge. When performed correctly, stewardship binds our high-gift donors to the organization and its mission, and they become invested in our success. When performed poorly, stewardship creates a gap, not filled through any other step and may lead to supporter dissatisfaction, distrust, and a degraded affiliation.

The Donor Giving Cycle

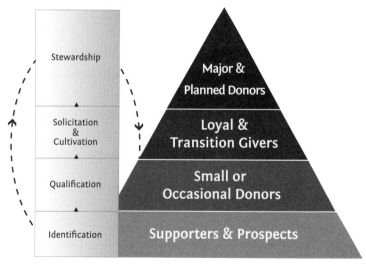

While actual giving motivations are different for each supporter, a connection to your vision and mission are the prime reasons that donors contribute. They feel passionate about your services, your programs, and your outcomes. They want to help those in need, have a desire to give back to others in the community, and generally want to make a difference in the world around them. Giving levels often increase with personal net worth, and some donors refer to increased tax incentives for motivation. We know that people give because they are asked. They also give because they are thanked. Regardless of the impetus, our contributors look for the reciprocating factor we call "stewardship" to keep the circular relationship in motion.

Both major and planned gift donors reside at the peak of the pyramid and will be your organization's transformational contributors.

Donor recognition must become more than a response to a gift or a response to a notification of an intended gift. In its purest form, donor recognition is a strategic tool for communicating with current and prospective donors. At its most genteel, it's a thoughtful relationship with your best friends. The methods of your stewardship program and the activities you perform in thanking those who fund your mission are the keys to enhanced giving, both now and in the future. Planned giving stewardship should follow these steps as well, even though the gift will be received some time — maybe not for a long time — in the future. Without this, your chances of getting and maintaining large planned gifts will remain outside your reach.

Who Should Be Part of Your Stewardship Program?

Planned gifts create both challenges and opportunities. When you are notified of a planned gift intention, it's easy to provide stewardship.

Unlike annual, capital, and major donors, however, there are many people who choose to remain silent. Some studies indicate this number may be four times, six times, or even 10 times greater than those who come forward.

Donors' reasons for anonymity are varied but tend to follow a basic theme: conservative values. Legacy donors do not regard themselves as wealthy, although many are. They worry about a secure future and do not consider their assets liquid. They also tend to shy away from highly public recognition and may even abhor it. Do not, however, confuse this with a lack of generosity or a desire to forgo all recognition and stewardship. Instead, it means we must be creative and expansive when considering stewardship for planned gift donors. It only benefits you to be as inclusive as possible with your targeted group. I suggest that you include the following characterizations in your prospect pool:

- Individuals that have already notified you of a planned, deferred, or legacy gift

- Donors of stocks, securities, and mutual fund shares no matter the amount of the gift

- All qualified inquirers of bequest language, gift annuity calculations, and information on life income gifts

- All board and committee members, professional-level staff members, and employees of 10 years or longer

- Donors who have made gifts at any level for 10 or more years or have given your organization 25 or more gifts including recurring/monthly gifts

- A minimum of 250 top planned giving prospects[5] identified through an analytics project or other vendor-related scoring

- All donors who have made single-year gifts of $10,000 or more

This "advanced" stewardship may seem unnatural, but it makes sense. Planned gifts to your organization are already in place, you just don't know of their existence. The groups noted above have the highest possibility of having already included you in an estate gift. Research indicates that bequest intentions shared prior to a donor's passing tend to be twice as large as bequests that were never revealed. Further, personal relationships cement the bequest gift. By thanking, reporting to, and accounting to these individuals in "advance" of their notification, you increase your chances that their planned gift is not only at the higher end but also that your organization is one of only several charitable beneficiaries.

Institutionalized Stewardship

It's your duty to woo these generous contributors into a comfortable situation where they can acknowledge their future intention, and you can do so by setting an example with your stewardship activities. An effective program has a number of components. However, donors and prospective donors expect certain common elements. While you can do many things to steward a gift, consider these fundamentals:

○ **Acknowledgement:** Your first response to a gift, any gift, should be to say "thank you." Be grateful. Say "thank you" in the most personal way possible. When it comes to thanking donors for their future planned gift, acknowledgement is critical. Use the least amount of "template" language feasible and include references that are specific to the donor's gift intention or desired outcome. Speak from the heart and consider a handwritten element. Additional acknowledgement from key players is also appropriate, for example, a faculty member, the vice president of programs, or a student. Every member of your staff — paid and volunteer leadership — should institutionalize donor stewardship, especially those at the top. Invite them to think of ways their role lends itself to saying "thank you." Induct them onto the gratitude team. Provide sample statements of appreciation that become part of their vocabulary. Ask them to say "thank you" to someone every day — and show your gratitude to them in return.

○ **Recognition:** With permission, recognize future gifts and annuity gifts in an upcoming publication, on your organization's website, and in your annual report. Not only is this an opportunity for natural contact, it is also another opportunity to be thankful. Be certain to provide access to the recognition piece or pieces. If your donor does not use the Internet or does not have access to a "members only" type of web page, provide an alternate document or hard copy issue.

○ **Accountability:** Report back to your donors, both future and current. Share the impact of similar gifts from other legacy donors that have already been put to work. Use detail and numbers to show your results. Create a communication piece that shows what role planned giving revenue plays for the year or for several past combined years. Highlight the total number of legacy givers of which you are aware. Use donor stories to bring your results to life.

○ **Access to Leadership:** When donors make significant gifts, they expect a little attention; some expect a lot! It's easy to provide it while also being cost-careful. Personal letters and summary reports from those in leadership positions cost nothing to write and have little or no cost to disseminate. If you already send your current major donors special mailings, notices, and invitations, add your legacy notifiers as well as your planned gift prospects to your list. Remember, the average bequest is more than $30,000 and surely qualifies this group as major givers. Begin to treat them in a manner in which you'd like them to become accustomed.

Special attention, in a group-like format, is usually welcomed and very appreciated.

○ **Celebrate:** Celebrations take many forms. Celebrate the notification of a planned gift when you receive it. Celebrate the anniversary of a charitable gift annuity and similar gifts each year on the signing date. Celebrate loyalty markers such as five or 10 years of giving or the 10th, 20th, 25th gift, and onward, no matter the amount of the gifts. Celebrate seasonal times of gratitude. Send hand-signed cards at Thanksgiving, at year-end, or even on Valentine's Day. Invite planned giving donors and prospects to your annual meeting, your kick-off, and ground-breaking events. The decision and expense to attend are the donors' responsibility, but the responsibility to extend the invitation is yours. Benefits and inner-circle activities such as these provide regular and strategic touch points with this future major donor group.

○ **Ongoing Stewardship Activities:** Create a comprehensive stewardship plan for your deferred gift donors. A touch every other month or so shows your continuing gratitude and welcoming disposition. Many planned gift donors may never accept an invitation to a meeting or even to have a cup of coffee. It's well known that this donor group is among the shyest of all — not in reality, but in activity. They tend to be modest and often do not see themselves as "philanthropists." Systematic touch points give these donors a sense of belonging but not of standing out.

Proactive stewardship of planned gift prospects creates the type of environment where gift notification seems natural. New planned gift donors already know and trust you and may feel comfortable enough to alert you to their deferred gift intentions.

11 Principles of Effective Stewardship

As you sit down to plan your legacy recognition, consider these 11 principles of stewardship provided by Kay Sprinkel Grace in her well-known book, *Beyond Fundraising*.[6]

1. Engage the donor immediately.

2. Don't mix messages, i.e., a thank-you note with an enclosed request for a gift.

3. Carve out a budget for stewardship — include personal outreach efforts as well as physical items.

4. Keep your stewardship in line with organizational image.

5. Determine what kind of involvement your planned giving donors want outside of making the donation.

6. Use current legacy notifiers to convey messages to potential planned gift donors; nothing speaks more volumes than a satisfied donor.

7. Tie your stewardship program to the mission.

8. Focus on intangible rather than tangible benefits — make donors into investors.

9. Maintain stewardship even if planned gift donors decrease or stop their current giving. Remember, the average planned gift is often many times larger than a donor's lifetime cumulative gifts.

10. Keep all donors part of your database unless they tell you otherwise.

11. Establish relationships between donors and program staff.

Assessing Your Own Stewardship Efforts

As a first step, you may want to assess your current stewardship efforts with your legacy donors and prospects. This quick checklist will get you started.

o Do you have a written plan?

o Does your plan include written, phone, and in-person components?

o Do you have a dedicated budget for stewardship?

o Do you look for ways to better acknowledge, recognize, and report to donors?

o Do you gather donor feedback?

o Do you network with others to exchange ideas?

o Do you gather examples of great stewardship components on a periodic basis?

o Do you encourage your colleagues to share their great stewardship ideas?

o Are you innovative and open for change?

Figure I shows a very simple example calendar of stewardship activities. As you begin to design your own program, be certain to include actions that reach out to your prospect pool as well. Steward them *in advance* of their gift notifications.

Timing	Stewardship Activity
January	"Informal Annual Report" — letter describing annual accomplishments and impact on your constituency
February	Annual update phone calls to all gift annuitants and charitable trust donors
April	Annual planned giving recognition event held
May	School year-end thank-you letter and photo from a graduating student
June	Annual phone calls to bequest intenders
July	Official annual report and donor listing with hand-signed letter from president

August	Mission component update report(s) from program director, dean, VP of research, etc.
October	Invitation to annual meeting mailed
November	Thanksgiving card to all known legacy donors
Ongoing	Anniversary cards, birthday cards
Monthly	New legacy society member packets
Weekly	Visit with one to two members of the legacy society

Figure I

In summary, strategic stewardship increases your organization's image, reputation, and priority with both current and future planned gift donors. Thoughtful gratitude and communication cost nothing. Take time to consider the rewards. One person per week who leaves you $70,000 as a final gift becomes $7,280,000 in just two years. If you start now, your future will be here before you know it.

---

[1] For the purpose of this paper, the term "planned gift" means any gift payable upon the donor's death.

[2] The terms "planned gift," "legacy gift," and "deferred gift" are used interchangeably herein.

[3] 15 x $70,000 = $1,050,000

[4] The terms "donor stewardship" and "donor recognition" are used interchangeably herein.

[5] For the purposes of this paper, "top planned giving prospects identified through an analytics project or other vendor-related scoring" should be selected using loyalty factors and not just using top scores. This provides a more diverse age group of prospects and does not focus on only older individuals. For more information on selecting your "top prospects" from a Target Analytics ProspectPoint project, contact the Target Analytics team at 800.468.8996, Option 5, and ask to speak with a team consultant.

[6] Kay Sprinkel Grace, Beyond Fundraising: New Strategies for Nonprofit Innovation and Investment (Wiley, 2005).

BONUS CHAPTER

Prospect Research for the Non-Researcher
by David Lamb

Good prospect research can mean the difference between receiving a large gift and a major gift. As many development officers know, when you improve your understanding of a prospect's wealth, interests, and stature in the community, you are better equipped to tailor your gift request more effectively to help the donor make the largest gift possible. But many organizations don't employ prospect researchers, which may force development officers to build their gift requests from a hunch. But as you will read in this chapter, this does not have to be the case! There are inexpensive tools — even free ones — available today that anyone can use to complete their own prospect research.

How to Go from Shooting in the Dark to Hitting Your Target

First, let's take a look at what types of tools you or your organization may lack so you can fill in the gaps to become more successful in targeting the right prospects and tailoring your asks.

What does the professional researcher have?

o   Time

o   Resources

o   Training

o   Experience

What do you have?

o   Personal knowledge of your organization's prospects — often not available to the professional researcher

o   Access to the same public information that everyone else has (including professional researchers)

o   A need to know some very specific information that will help you prioritize your prospects

What do you need to know?

o   Where do your prospects live? Do they own property?

o   Where do your prospects work? How does their employment contribute to their ability to give?

o   Do your prospects make gifts? If so, how big?

o   How and where are your prospects connected in the community?

Obviously, the list of what you need to know could go on and on. But it's easy — and dangerous — to get so wrapped up in your prospect research that you talk to fewer prospects. For major gift fundraisers, it is better to err on spending more time in the field and less time behind the desk. Still, there are some things you can discover with some basic resources that can help you prioritize your prospects and more effectively engage them.

Don't expect to be able to discover someone's net worth or to be able to find the same amount of information on all of your prospects.

However, what you can find may help you focus your energies more strategically. Consider the following scenario: You have two donors who have made equal, moderately large gifts recently but are otherwise unknown to you. By "moderately large," I mean a gift that wouldn't be considered a major gift, but is larger than a typical gift — large enough to get your attention. For donor #1, you can discover that she owns an $800,000 home and gave $5,000 in political gifts last year. For donor #2, you learn that he owns a $250,000 home, but you are unable to discover any information about his past giving.

For major gift fundraisers, it is better to err on spending more time in the field and less time behind the desk.

Let's acknowledge that this situation is a simplified one, and it doesn't take into account some of the other factors that may exist below the surface. It's possible that these prospects might be equally capable of making major gifts, or that the one who seems wealthier might be more burdened with debt or owns a home that has lost considerable value in a troubled real estate market. But the evidence suggests that donor #1 may have greater resources than the second. Your time and energy is also a limited resource, so if you had to choose which prospect to try and contact for a personal thank-you and follow-up, the evidence favors donor #1.

Here are some resources that a fundraiser can consult when prioritizing a list of prospects. These tools need to be free or low cost and involve a minimum amount of time and effort. You also need to understand that nothing comes without a price — even if it doesn't cost you money. You will need to put in some time to make use of these tools, but for the right prospects, it will be time well spent. That said, it is a good idea to put a limit on that time so that you don't get locked in what is called "analysis paralysis." As you are beginning to become familiar with these resources, you might need a couple of hours per prospect. However, as your proficiency increases, you should try to find out what you can in an hour or less per prospect, then get out on the road.

Real Estate

Real estate can be a useful gauge of a prospect's overall wealth. The neighborhood in which a family lives tends to reflect economic status. There are exceptions, of course, but as a broad economic indicator, real estate value is a good starting point.

Fortunately, the value of virtually every property in the country is public information. You can often access this information through the website for the tax assessor of the county where the property is located. Each county may have a slightly different set of search options to find your prospect's property. In many cases, you can search by name, name and address, or just address.

There are at least two things you should know about your prospect's home: what is its assessed (taxable) value and what is its market value? The place to start is the county assessor where the property is located. You can often find the county assessor's website at one of these two websites: www.pulawski.net or publicrecords.netronline.com.

If you don't know the county for the address you're searching, look it up at the U.S. Postal Service ZIP code site zip4.usps.com/zip4/welcome.jsp. This will give you the full address in standard format. To the right of that address, you'll see a link to "mailing industry information," which will tell you the county for that address.

The county assessor website will provide the tax — or assessed — value of the property. It may also provide lots of additional helpful information that may include the market value, a history of sales, and a description of the property.

Tax value and market value can be quite different. If the assessor doesn't provide a market value, you might be able to get an approximation of the market value at www.zillow.com.

Are you willing to spend a little money? The website KnowX, www.KnowX.com, allows you to search by name within a state or within the country to find information about people and assets. The advantage here is that you don't have to know your prospect's address in order to find not only their home but other property they may own as well. Avoid this, though, if your prospect has a common name. Retrieving a single property record from this website is fairly inexpensive.

Donations

Political donations made to candidates for national office — or political action committees that support those candidates — are reported by the Federal Election Commission. There are limits on the size of donation that is allowed, so these donations are not necessarily a good indication of a donor's capacity. Nevertheless, it is possible for a political donor to give up to $115,500 to a combination of candidates, PACs, and party committees in a two-year campaign cycle. It isn't common for someone to max out his or her donation capacity on political donations. Even though a political gift is not considered a charitable gift, political donations — even small ones — are evidence of giving behavior. Further, there is a strong correlation between political giving and charitable giving.

A side benefit of finding political donations is that the document reporting the gift (yes, you can download an image of the gift record) often includes the donor's home address, employer, and business title.

There are many sources for this information. One of the easiest to use is <u>herndon1.sdrdc.com/fecimg/norindsea.html</u>. Simply enter a person's name to discover if any gifts are reported. The city where the donor lives is also listed to help sort out your prospect from others with the same name in different cities.

Willing to spend a little money? Charitable donations are not reported through a central clearinghouse like political donations are, but several companies have amassed large databases of charitable contributions by copying the donor lists from annual reports and honor rolls of donors published by nonprofit organizations. With more than 41 million donation records, NOZA, <u>www.nozasearch.com</u>, has the largest database. It can be searched by donor name and filtered by state, city, and donation year. Other resources like DonorBank have become great places to get charitable giving data as well.

Public Company Insiders

The only people who are required by law to disclose their stock holdings are public company insiders. These are directors, top officers, and 10% shareholders of publicly traded companies. The good news is that, if your constituent is an insider, you can learn specific value information of this very gift-able asset. The bad news is that only a tiny fraction of your constituency is likely to have insider status.

Insiders are very easy to research. There are several different websites you can search for insider data for free. I recommend J3 Information Services Group's Insider Reports tool: <u>www.j3sg.com</u>. On the home page, look for Quick Search, then enter your prospect's name into the Insider Reports box, and click "Go". If no information comes back, your prospect is probably not an insider.

Other Professionals

While many public company insiders are major gift prospects, most major gift prospects are not insiders. They are owners and leaders of business. They are professionals like doctors or lawyers. In many cases, these "millionaires next door" are very difficult to spot in your database or in the public information sources. If, however, you have a reason to believe that someone might be able to give more than they do now, here are some places to look for professional information:

o   Lawyers: Martindale-Hubbell (www.martindale.com)

o   Doctors: AMA DocFinder (webapps.ama-assn.org/doctorfinder/html/patient.jsp)

o   ZoomInfo: General professionals automatically compiled from Internet sources (www.zoominfo.com)

o   LinkedIn: A social networking site for professionals (www.linkedin.com)

o   Hoovers: A business directory searchable by executive name (www.hoovers.com/free)

Keep in mind that sources like ZoomInfo and LinkedIn, and even Hoovers to some degree, are not verified by a disinterested third party. Usually, self reported information (as in LinkedIn) is very accurate, but it is also possible for someone to misrepresent him or herself. These caveats should apply to almost any data source in existence:

o   Every source contains old or inaccurate information to some degree

o   You get what you pay for

Most of what is described here is free or relatively inexpensive. You can find many additional useful resources, both free and those that charge a fee, at my research website: www.lambresearch.com.

Income

Unless your prospect is an insider officer in a public company, you will almost certainly not find a definitive report of his or her salary. In some cases, however, it is possible to estimate constituents' income based on what else you know about them. Salary surveys abound and are easy to access over the Internet. Two good ones are www.salary.com and www.jobs-salary.com.

What Do You Do with All the Information?

Estimating a prospect's giving capacity is a mixture of art, science, and relationship. There is no magic formula that can be applied with confidence and accuracy in every case. You, as a development officer, are very aware of the relationship component. Adding research data injects some science into the equation. In the end, you must establish the ask amount based on what the prospect has told you, what others who know the prospect have told you, and what your research has told you. Evidence of large gifts that the prospect has made suggests that the prospect could give a large gift again. Ownership of semi-liquid assets such as stock suggests a gift vehicle. If a person owns expensive property, it probably hints at assets beyond the property itself. In a wealthy family's portfolio, real estate is not usually the largest asset. Additionally, we can't discount the possibility that a property — other than the prospect's home — might be the gift itself.

The goal of your research is not to pin down the prospect's net worth, but to appropriately rank the prospect's potential in comparison to other prospects so that you can spend your time with the prospects that are most capable and likely to give larger gifts.

Various rules of thumb may be useful when rating a prospect's capacity. But remember that none of these will precisely fit your prospect's situation. They are only guides to get you started in the right direction. Then you refine your ask based on what you know of the prospect's circumstances and your development instincts.

A prospect may give 5% to 10% of annual income. To attempt to compute this, here are some equations that can help:

o   Total real estate value x 4 x 5% (use only when real estate value is over $500,000)

o   Total stock holdings x 4 x 5% (use only when known stock value is over $100,000)

o   5% of total known assets (use only when asset value is near or over $1 million)

Willing to Spend a Little Money?

So far, I've asked this question in connection with specific kinds of searches: real estate or donations. You can get a lot of information for free, but by paying a small fee, you can get some advantages in search options and data quality. You trade time and efficiency for money. Often the fee is small enough to make the time-savings worth the cost.

Organizations known as data aggregators have been on the scene for a few years. These companies make several sources searchable simultaneously. A researcher or development officer can enter some basic name, address, and business information and have the computer simultaneously search several of the sites that are mentioned here plus others that would be prohibitively expensive for the small shop because of the subscriptions required. A few minutes after submitting the search, a profile is delivered with information about real estate, company affiliations, insider stockholdings, nonprofit affiliations, donations, and biographical data. It's a big time saver.

The company I work for, Target Analytics, provides this data aggregation service for a fee based on your needs including the number of searches you need and how you want to receive or store the data.

Ultimately, you may decide that there are some prospects where the services of a professional researcher are really needed to help you with some of your best prospects. You might not need to hire a researcher — perhaps you can rent one. Hire a freelancer to do profiles on specific prospects. You can find a list of qualified researchers here: <u>home. comcast.net/~lambresearch/OtherPages.htm#ResearchFirms</u>.

Why Not Start with Google®?

It does seem like the obvious starting place, doesn't it? Want to find a movie review? Google® it. Want to learn how to make a brick wall? Google® it. Many casual users of the Internet start their research with Google®. However, experienced researchers know that there is a large portion of the Internet that is invisible to Google®. It is better to start your research with more targeted sources like the ones mentioned in this chapter. Once you know more about your prospect, you can add more intelligent key words to your Google® search, which you should do at the end of your research, not the beginning.

Happy researching!

NOTES

ABOUT THE AUTHORS

Frank Barry
Manager, Professional Services

Frank Barry manages professional services for Blackbaud Internet Solutions and is responsible for driving performance in the consulting, technical services, and project management practices. His team is focused on delivering quality work and repeatable solutions to ensure customers are successful using Blackbaud's Internet products. Frank joined Blackbaud in 2004 as a project manager. In 2007, he began managing the enterprise implementation team. With more than eight years of experience in the nonprofit arena, he has worked with a diverse group of organizations including prominent churches and universities. Prior to working at Blackbaud, Frank worked in the San Diego, California region of an international church. His responsibilities included running web initiatives (website, CRM, email) and youth ministry activities. Frank received his bachelor's degree in computer science from San Diego State University.

Lawrence Henze, J.D.
Managing Director, Target Analytics

Lawrence Henze, managing director of Target Analytics, has extensive experience in fundraising, market research, and the application of predictive modeling services to the nonprofit marketplace. The founder of Core Data Services, which Blackbaud acquired in 2001, he has also served as vice president of predictive modeling services at USA Group Noel Levitz and president of The Philanthropic Division of Econometrics, Inc. Lawrence has 15 years of experience in development, raising more than $125 million, primarily for higher education institutions. During his career, he has personally reviewed the giving histories of more than 30,000 planned givers across the country. He holds a bachelor's degree in political science from Carroll College in Wisconsin, and a master's degree in public policy and administration and a law degree from the University of Wisconsin at Madison.

ABOUT THE AUTHORS

David Lamb
Senior Consultant, Target Analytics

David Lamb joined Blackbaud in 2004 following three years as an independent consultant for prospect research. David has more than 20 years of experience in the prospect research field. His Prospect Research Page (www.lambresearch.com) is a trusted and popular resource among prospect researchers. David is a frequent speaker at professional conferences, including those sponsored by the Council for Advancement and Support of Education (CASE), The Association of Fundraising Professionals (AFP), and The Association of Professional Researchers for Advancement (APRA). His areas of expertise include prospect research, prospect management, fundraising, and database systems. In 1997, he received APRA's Service Award for outstanding service to the profession, and in 2001, he was awarded the CASE Steuben Apple Award for excellence in teaching. He holds a bachelor's degree in sociology from Sterling College (Sterling, Kansas), a master's degree in sociology from Wichita State University, and a master's degree in divinity from San Francisco Theological Seminary.

Katherine Swank, J.D.
Consultant, Target Analytics

Katherine Swank joined the Target Analytics team in 2007 with more than 25 years of legal and nonprofit management experience. Prior to joining Target Analytics, she was the national director of gift planning at the National Multiple Sclerosis Society, where she provided fundraising consulting services to the Society's chapter leadership and development staff for six years. Katherine has raised more than $215 million during her career, with a focus on planned and major giving. As an affiliate faculty member of Regis University's Masters in Global Nonprofit Leadership program in Denver, Katherine teaches classroom and online courses on wealth and philanthropy in America. In 2010, Katherine was inducted into Target Analytics' Hall of Fame, which recognizes team members that epitomize excellence in service. She earned a bachelor's degree in counseling and education from the University of Northern Colorado and a Doctor of Jurisprudence from Drake University Law School in Des Moines, Iowa.

ABOUT BLACKBAUD AND THE
DESKTOP REFERENCE SERIES

Blackbaud is the leading global provider of software and services designed specifically for nonprofit organizations, enabling them to improve operational efficiency, build strong relationships, and raise more money to support their missions. Approximately 22,000 organizations — including University of Arizona Foundation, American Red Cross, Cancer Research UK, The Taft School, Lincoln Center, In Touch Ministries, Tulsa Community Foundation, Ursinus College, Earthjustice, International Fund for Animal Welfare, and the WGBH Educational Foundation — use one or more Blackbaud products and services for fundraising, constituent relationship management, financial management, website management, direct marketing, education administration, ticketing, business intelligence, prospect research, consulting, and analytics. Since 1981, Blackbaud's sole focus and expertise has been partnering with nonprofits and providing them the solutions they need to make a difference in their local communities and worldwide. Headquartered in the United States, Blackbaud also has operations in Australia, Canada, Hong Kong, the Netherlands, and the United Kingdom. Target Analytics, a division of Blackbaud, is the leading provider of comprehensive analytics solutions for donor acquisition, prospect research, fundraising performance, and collaborative peer benchmarking to help nonprofits maximize fundraising results at every stage of the donor lifecycle.

Look for more relevant topics in our Desktop Reference series, or visit www.blackbaud.com/DesktopReference for other valuable tools and information.